COATBRIDGE HIGH SCHOOL

C - H - S

LABORARE EST PRECARE

Session 19*30* - 19*81*

Prize

awarded to

Katherine H. Douglas

for excellence in

French

in Class **4**

JOHN G. FORSYTH, *Rector.*

THE SEASONS

Louis Lawrence

Foreword by Roy Strong

Webb & Bower

EXETER, ENGLAND

Published in Great Britain 1981 by
Webb & Bower (Publishers) Limited
33 Southernhay East, Exeter, Devon EX1 1NS

Designed by Peter Wrigley

British Library Cataloguing in Publication Data
Lawrence, Louis
   The Seasons.
   1. Lawrence, Louis
   2. Seasons in art
   3. Seasons - Literary collections
   4. English literature
   I. Title
   741.9/42   NC242/L36.
   ISBN 906671-22-1

Printed and bound in Italy by Arnoldo Mondadori Editore

FOREWORD

Roy Strong

The Seasons was compiled between the years 1887 and 1890 by Louis Lawrence, a publicity artist for Maws, the London chemist. He died an old man in 1945 so that what we have is a work of his youth, the efforts of someone in his late teens in the year of Queen Victoria's Golden Jubilee. There is nothing to indicate that it was the product of an artist with any art-school training, but rather of someone who was learning by way of apprenticeship and by copying what he saw around him. And in this lies part of its peculiar charm.

What sort of setting does *The Seasons* spring from and why does it cast a spell? Its milieu is the modest moral world of late Victorian lower middle-class life with its evangelical piety, its cultivation of God expressed in nature, its sentiment for hearth and home and the virtues of family life. It therefore epitomizes for us a lost security romanticized by living memory that can just about reach that far back. The essence of the book is, of course, its texts. Tennyson, Longfellow, Shelley and Scott are quoted, but there are also the "many others" to whom Lawrence refers, totally forgotten purveyors of morally uplifting verse for the family: the Rev. R. Wilton, Mary Eugenia, the Rev. A.A. Graley or H.P. Spofford. The tradition of this type of poetry we catch in its death-throes today in Christmas card verses which continue to reveal the strength of the hold of this formula that interlocked pictured image and virtuous thought in lyric form.

The Seasons is an offspring of that ethos. It belongs to the atmosphere of home life before the advent of the car, radio or television. Family entertainment consisted in reading, making music and hobbies, all of which were edited down once a week to those activities regarded as suitable for the Lord's Day. *The Seasons* is essentially a Sunday book. M.V. Hughes in the first volume of her trilogy entitled *A London Child of the 1870s* recalls that on that day "all amusements, as well as work, were forbidden. It was a real privation not to be allowed to draw and paint. However, an exception was made in favour of illuminated texts . . .". One can visualize *The Seasons* being the result of just such a situation.

It also reflects another late Victorian phenomenon, the holiday, the railways opening up England to classes of society that before had never travelled for leisure. The beauties of nature and the picturesque charm of town and village are what the guidebooks dwell upon. Lawrence obviously frequented the Isle of Wight, first made fashionable by Victoria and Albert. In *The Seasons* the village of Bonchurch, close to Ventnor, figures with its pond, as well as Carisbrook Castle and Shanklin. Hastings and Dover, both easily accessible by rail, appear, and views of Lynmouth, first eulogized by Southey, St Mawgan-in-Pydar, near Newquay and Land's End were surely the result of holidays in Devon and Cornwall. The subject-matter throughout embodies the visual repertory of both guidebook and postcard: waterfall and windmill, sunset and stormy sea, rocky cliffhead and meandering river. And always, interspersed, nature study in the form of birds and sprays of flowers.

Compilations of this kind are quintessential expressions of the spread of literacy after the Education Act of 1870. The boom that followed in the production of new magazines and newspapers to feed this mass market was unprecedented. It was the era of the monthly illustrated magazine with its serialized novel. For the class of society to which Lawrence belonged such publications would have been the first initial contact with any form of graphic art and with this we can neatly place *The Seasons* in context. The composition of these pages with their picturesque topographical views, vignettes and contrived alphabets come directly out of a tradition of page layout combining text and illustration, established by Herbert Ingram in the *Illustrated London News* during the 1840s and '50s. John Gilbert was the head of a team of artists who created this style where the Victorian reader would find the content of the text expressed in the steel engravings. In an early issue of the magazine some rural scenes by Birket Foster, clearly a great influence on Lawrence, are accompanied by an exposition of these principles which read almost like a guide to those for *The Seasons*:

> Each bears the aspect of the month - a sort of pictured climatology, with the natural appearances of the season, and the monthly phases of the farmer's life. Thus, in January, the ground and roofs are thickly mantled with snow, the effect of which, against the black wintry sky, and the bare bough trees, is very telling; the scene is a farmyard, where the feeding of poultry, pigs and cattle, seems to break the sleep and silence of the season; the contrast of the still and busy life is excellent. The tail-piece is a shepherd carrying one of his flock in a snowstorm. The business of February is ploughing and sowing; the rooks are building, and all nature is just astir . . .

Lawrence's book is exactly like this, although he generally avoids figures and animals because they quickly reveal the limits of his capabilities. Lettering and landscape are his forte, although the charm of the book resides to a great extent in its amateur naivety. I have no doubt that a great many of the illustrations are directly lifted or reworked from contemporary magazines, nearly all of which featured seasonal lyrics and vignettes, but that in the end is not the point. It is the modesty, domesticity and the unquestioned sense of duty and values in this book that, a century later, most appeal to us. Doggerel the verse may often be but how evocative of the ethos of a period and of the man who was moved to compile this book.

While the earth remaineth, seed-time and harvest, and cold and heat, and summer and winter, and day and night shall not cease.

Genesis, VIII 22.

All thy works shall give thanks unto thee, O Lord; and thy saints shall bless thee.

Psalm 145 10. R.V.

SPRING.

SUMMER.

AUTUMN.

WINTER.

L.C.L.

The Poems are by

M. Howitt,   M. R. Jarvis,   H. W. Longfellow,

J. Montgomery,   R. Southey,   W. Scott,

A. Tennyson,   R. Wilton,   W. Wordsworth,

Major W. A. H. Sigourney,

and many others.

The drawings are by

Louis Göttfried Lawrence.

1887 —— 1890.

ST. PETER'S,
BROADSTAIRS.

THE
SEASONS.

SPRING.

Ten thousand different
flowers
To Thee sweet offerings bear;
And cheerful birds, in shady
bowers,
Sing forth Thy tender care.

The fields on every side,
The trees on every hill,
The glorious sun,
the rolling tide,
Proclaim Thy wonders still.

But trees, and fields, and
skies,
Still praise a God unknown;
For gratitude and love can
rise
From living hearts alone.

These living hearts of ours,
Thy holy name would bless;
The blossoms of ten thousand
flowers
Would please the Saviour less.

While earth itself
decays,
Our souls can never die,
Oh, tune them all to
sing Thy praise
In better songs on high.

Blue-bells.

May-Blossom.

Spring-evening.

The roseate hues of
early dawn,
The brightness of
the day,
The crimson of the
sunset sky,
How fast they fade away!
Oh, for the pearly gates
of heaven,
Oh, for the golden floor,
Oh, for the Sun of right-
eousness
That setteth nevermore!

Lo, the winter
is past,.....
The flowers appear on the earth;
The time of the singing of birds is come.

The Song of Songs.
Solomon, II. 11 & 12.

The winter time departeth;
The early flowers expand;
The blackbird and the turtle-dove
Are heard throughout the land.

Before us lies
the Spring-time —
Thank God, the time
of mirth —
When birds are singing
in the trees,
And flowers gem
all the earth.

M. HOWITT.

"THE West wind has breathed
                through the woodlands,
The sun lingereth lovingly there—
And the trees in a tremulous waking

Have clothed them in garments so fair
      That we wander with hearts light as
                childhood can know,
And feel that God's Heaven is round us below."

E. DAWSON.

" Thou blessest the

springing thereof. "

Thou makest the outgoings of the morning and evening to rejoice. Thou visitest the earth, and waterest it; the river of God is full of water: Thou providest them corn, when Thou hast so prepared the earth. Thou waterest her furrows abundantly; Thou settlest the ridges thereof: Thou makest it soft with showers; Thou blessest the springing thereof. Thou crownest the year with Thy goodness; and Thy paths drop fatness. They drop upon the pastures of the wilderness: and the hills are girded with joy. The pastures are clothed with flocks; the valleys also are covered over with corn; they shout for joy, they also sing."

Psalms, 65: 8-13. R.V.

What change is this
    that o'er the
        world appears?
It was but yesterday
    that all was tears
And sadness, and
        despair,
and wintry fears.

Now music of young
    voices fills the air;
    Grief is no more, and joy is everywhere;
        Colour and bloom where all was brown and bare!

Birds on the budding hedges sing and sway;
        The happy sunlight

                    fills the joyous day;
            And skies are blue that first were dull
                        and grey!

            White clouds their fleeting
                        shadows lightly fling
                O'er breezy upland
                        pastures; everything
                Rejoices with the re-arisen Spring.

            Earth breaks the trammels of her
                        frost-bound prison,
            And after Winter's death finds life anew.

        Courage, faint heart! Awake! Thy Spring
                    is risen,
        Thou hast thy time of resurrection too.

                            Helen Maud Waithman.

"Not worlds on worlds in phalanx deep,
  Need we to prove a God is here;
The daisy, fresh from Nature's sleep,
  Tells of His hand in lines as clear.
For who but He who arched the skies,
  And pours the day-spring's living flood,
Wondrous alike in all He tries,
  Could raise the daisy's crimson bud,
  And fling it, unrestrained and free,
  O'er hill and dale, and desert sod,
That man, where'er he walks, may see
  In every step the stamp of God!"

Good.

"Where thick thy primrose
        blossoms play,
Lovely and innocent as they,
  O'er coppice, lawns,
        and dells,
In bands the rural
    children stray,
  To pluck thy nectared
        bells."

Montgomery.

To the Cuckoo.

O blithe new-comer! I have heard,
    I hear thee and rejoice.
O Cuckoo! shall I call thee bird,
    Or but a wandering voice?

While I am lying on the grass,
    Thy twofold shout I hear,
From hill to hill it seems to pass,
    At once far off and near.

Though babbling only, to the vale,
    Of sunshine and of flowers,
Thou bringest unto me a tale
    Of visionary hours.

Thrice welcome, darling of the spring!
    Even yet thou art to me
No bird: but an invisible thing,
    A voice, a mystery.

The same whom in my school-boy days
    I listened to; that cry
Which made me look a thousand ways
    In bush, and tree, and sky.

To seek thee did I
        often rove
    Through woods and
            on the green;
    And thou wert still a hope,
        a love;
    Still longed for, never seen.

    And I can listen to thee yet;
        Can lie upon
                the plain
        And listen, till I do beget
            That golden time again.

O blessed bird!
    the earth we pace
Again appears
        to be
An unsubstantial
        faëry place;
    That is fit home
        for thee!

        W. Wordsworth.

"When Spring unlocks the flowers, to paint the laughing soil,

When Summer's balmy showers refresh the mower's toil,

When Winter binds in frosty chains the fallow and the flood—

In God the earth rejoiceth still, and owns its

Maker good.

* * * *

The flowers of Spring may wither,
the hope of Summer fade,
The Autumn droop in Winter, the birds
forsake the shade;
The wind be lulled,
the sun and moon
forget their old decree,
But we
in nature's latest hour,
O Lord!
will cling
to Thee."

Forget-me-Nots.

Weirdlaw Hill.

Weirdlaw Hill.

"The sun upon the Weirdlaw Hill,
    In Ettrick's vale, is sinking sweet;
The westland wind is hushed and still,
    The lake lies sleeping at my feet.
Yet not the landscape to mine eye
    Bears those sweet hues that once it bore;
Though Evening, with her richest dye,
    Flames o'er the hills of Ettrick shore."

Walter Scott.

The Sky-lark.

Oh, warn away the gloomy night! With music make the welkin ring; Bird of the dawn!
on joyful wing, Soar through thine element of light, Till nought in heaven mine
eye can see, Except the morning star and thee.

But speech of mine can ne'er reveal Secrets so freely told above; Yet is
their burden joy and love, And all the bliss a bird can feel, Whose wing in
heaven to earth is bound, Whose home and heart are on the ground.

Unlike the lark be thou, my friend! No downward cares thy
thoughts engage; But, in thine house of pilgrimage, Though
from the ground thy songs ascend, Still be their burden
joy and love! Heaven is thy home, thy heart above.

Oh, welcome in the cheerful day! Through rosy clouds
the shades retire; The sun hath touched thy plumes
with fire, And girt thee with a golden ray;
Now shape and voice are vanished quite,
Nor eye nor ear can track their flight.

Might I translate thy strain, and give
Words to thy notes in human
tongue, The sweetest lay that
e'er I sung, The lay that
would the longest live, I
should record upon this
page, And sing thy
song from age to age.

J. Montgomery.

Violets.

Arethusa.

"Arethusa arose
From her couch of snows
In the Acroceraunian mountains,—
From cloud and from crag
with many a jag,
Shepherding her bright fountains.
She leapt down the rocks
with her rainbow locks
Streaming among the
streams;

Her steps paved with green
          the downward ravine
Which slopes to the western gleams;
     And gliding and springing
               she went, ever singing;
In murmurs as soft as sleep;
     The earth seemed to love her,
          and heaven smiled above her,
               As she lingered towards the deep."

P. B. Shelley.

It is not always May.

The sun is bright, the air is clear,
    The darting swallows soar
               and sing,
And from the stately elms I hear
    The blue-bird prophesying Spring.

So blue yon winding river flows,
    It seems an outlet from the sky,
Where, waiting till the west wind blows,
    The freighted clouds at anchor lie.

All things are new;— the buds, the leaves,
    That gild the elm-tree's nodding crest,
And ev'n the nest beneath the eaves;—
    There are no birds in last year's nest!

All things rejoice in youth and love,
    The fulness of their first delight!
And learn from the soft heavens above
    The melting tenderness of night.

Maiden,
    that read'st
        this simple rhyme,
Enjoy thy youth,
        it will not stay;
Enjoy the fragrance
            of thy prime,
For O! it is not always May!

Enjoy the Spring of
            Love and Youth,
    To some good angel
            leave the rest;
For time will teach thee
                soon the truth,
There are no birds in last year's nest!

H. W. Longfellow.

THE CHAFFINCH.

The Chaffinch

takes his summer rest
Among the fruit or forest trees,
Or in the hawthorn builds his nest,
Secure from pilfering enemies.

Aye welcome is his song, and when
Its early notes break on the ear,
A gladness fills the hearts of men,—
Their souls grow blithe with hopeful cheer;
For well they know it heralds Spring,
With buds and blossoms on her wing!
Come, then, O joyous bird, and be
The herald of a new-born glee,
The messenger of happy hours,
Of sunny skies and leafy bowers.

Hail, smiling morn!

Hail, smiling morn,
That tips the hills with gold,
Whose rosy fingers ope the gates of day,
Who the gay face of Nature doth unfold,
At whose bright presence darkness flies away.

"When from the opening chambers of the east
The morning springs, in thousand liveries drest,
The early larks their morning tribute pay,
And, in shrill notes, salute the blooming day.
Refreshèd fields with pearly dew do shine,
And tender blades therewith their tops incline.
Their painted leaves the unblown flowers expand,
And with their odorous breath perfume the land."

J. Thomson.

In the morning will I direct
my prayer unto Thee,
and will look up.

Psalm. 5: 3.

'If in the field I meet a smiling flower,
    Methinks it whispers,
            "God created me,
And I to Him devote my little hour,
    In lonely sweetness
            and humility."'

J. MONTGOMERY.

L.G. LAWRENCE.

SUMMER.

Summer.

How beautiful is summer when the bee is on the wing,
And on the clustering hazel boughs the linnets sit and sing;
Bright gladsome days of sunshine, the weary heart to cheer,
And chase the shades of sadness from the anxious brow of care.

How beautiful the fields in their jewelled robe of green,
And the cool and shady lanes where the sun is seldom seen;
Where at eve we love to wander and breathe the scented air,
Perfumed with sweetest odour from the honeysuckle there.

A BREEZY MORNING.

How beautiful the billows that toss their foam on high,
And the placid lake reposing
beneath a cloudless sky;
The sparkling silver fountain in the cool delicious shade,
And the lowly streamlet murmuring
through the green and verdant glade.

How beautiful the happy homes
where England's sons
are reared,
But more happy still and hallowed
where God is loved and feared;
Where at morning and at evening
is heard the voice of prayer,
Commending every loved one to a
Father's tender care.

MARY EUGENIA.

AT SHANKLIN I.W.

It is summer! it is summer!
...how beautiful it looks!
There is sunshine on the old gray hills,
and sunshine on the brooks,
A singing-bird on every bough,
soft perfumes on the air,
A happy smile
on each young lip,
and gladness everywhere.

M. Howitt.

"Clear had the day been from the dawn,
All chequered was the sky,
Thin clouds like scarfs
of cobweb lawn
Veiled heaven's most
glorious eye.
The wind had no more
strength than this,
That leisurely
it blew,
To make one leaf
the next to kiss
That closely
by it grew."

M. Drayton.

In the Sunshine

"Live in the sunshine," the skylark
   Giving a voice   is singing,
     to the glad summer day;
Out of the azure his clear notes
      are ringing—
"Live in the sunshine, and sing
     while you may."

Clover and daisy-moons, high in
Breathe   the meadows,
    the same secret of living aright,
  Lifting their bright heads afar
       from the shadows—
"Live in the sunshine and grow in the light."

So sings the brooklet, the hillside adorning, Flashing and sparkling with beauty aglow—
Live in the sunshine and filled with the morning, Carry its brightness wherever you go!"

God of the sunshine, its Maker and Giver, Who to Thine own art a sun and a shield,
  Teach us, we pray Thee, by song-bird and river,
     Help us to live as the flowers of the field.

Give us a heart to be trusting and cheerful,
  When in the shadows Thy love hath allowed:
And should our weak faith be downcast and fearful,
  Doubting Thy mercy when under the cloud—

Light of the wide world, arise for our healing,
  Scatter our gloom with the sunbeams
       of grace;
Shine on us, Lord, and Thy glory revealing,
  Make us to dwell in the light of Thy face!

MARY ROWLES JARVIS.

STAY near me—
        do not take thy flight!
    A little longer stay in sight!
        Much converse do I find in thee,
        Historian of my infancy!
    Float near me; do not yet depart!
    Dead times revive in thee:
            Thou bring'st, gay creature as
                        thou art!
        A solemn image to my heart,
        My father's family!

    Oh! pleasant, pleasant were the days,
    The time, when, in our childish plays,
            My sister Emmeline and I
            Together chased the butterfly!
    A very hunter did I rush
    Upon the prey:—with leaps and springs
            I followed on from brake to bush;
            But she, God love her! feared to brush
    The dust from off its wings.

                            W. Wordsworth.

There is an hour
      in Summer's
            busy day
When Nature seems to
pause, and over all
      Comes a brief
sleep, hush'd with
            the lullaby
Of myriad insects'
wings, and now
      some small
            bird's call.

The earth lies trembling
      'neath the sun's fierce ray,
The reapers slumber in the
            shade; and soon
Some little village church-bell, far away,
      Slowly and dreamily strikes the
                  hour of noon.

Soft—in the hush of noontide, as we stand,
      The waking world a dreamland's fantasy—
There comes a whisper from the far-off land,
      Bringing us nearer to great Nature's
                  mystery.
'Twas here—'tis gone; the reaper
                  whets his scythe:
      We hear the talk of men,
                  the hum of bees—
The world's awake again, the
                  birds sing blythe;
      How bright the river gleams
                  between the trees!

G. C.

Reflections.

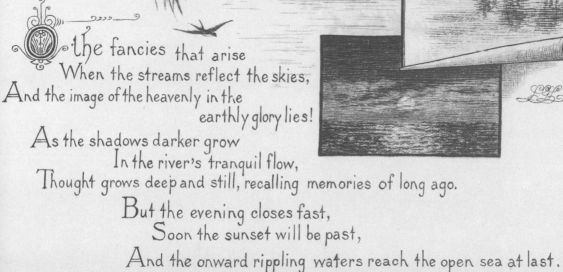

O the fancies that arise
When the streams reflect the skies,
And the image of the heavenly in the
earthly glory lies!

As the shadows darker grow
In the river's tranquil flow,
Thought grows deep and still, recalling memories of long ago.

But the evening closes fast,
Soon the sunset will be past,
And the onward rippling waters reach the open sea at last.

M. R.

THE GULL

"Happy seabirds! how they hover
O'er yon headland's
breezy crest,
And their tender nestlings cover
With warm wing and downy breast.

Happy seabirds! gliding, glancing,
Through the livelong summer day,
Where the merry waves are dancing
In the broad and sunny bay.

Lovely birds! with graceful motion
Giving life to rock and sand,
Adding beauty to the ocean,
Adding beauty to the strand.

How the eye delights to follow
Where they circle o'er the deep,
Or with swiftness of the swallow
O'er the glassy waters sweep."

Rev. R. Wilton. M.A.

"How dear to me the hour when daylight dies,
And sunbeams melt along the silent sea;

For then sweet dreams of other days arise,
And memory breathes her vesper sigh to thee."

J. Moore.

Near the Source.

The Brook.

I come from haunts
    of coot and hern,
  I make a sudden sally,
    And sparkle out
      among the fern,
  To bicker down
    a valley.

By thirty hills I hurry down,
  Or slip between the ridges,
By twenty thorps, a little town,
  And half a hundred bridges.

Till last by Philip's farm I flow
  To join the brimming river,
For men may come and men may go,
  But I go on for ever.

I chatter over
  stony ways,
In little sharps and
      trebles,
  I bubble into eddying bays,
    I babble on the pebbles.

Rustic Bridge.
Lynmouth.

With many a curve my banks I fret
    By many a field and fallow,
    And many a fairy foreland set
    With willow-weed and mallow.

    I chatter, chatter, as I flow
    To join the
        brimming river,
    For men may come
        and men may go,
    But I go on
        for ever.

I wind about, and in
                    and out,
    With here
            a blossom sailing,
And here and there
                a lusty trout,
    And here and there
                    a grayling,

            And here
                and there
                        a foamy flake
            Upon me,
                    as I travel
            With many a silvery
                            waterbreak
            Above the golden
                            gravel,

            And draw
                them all along,
                            and flow
            To join the
                    brimming river,
            For men may come
                        and men may go,
            But I go on for ever.

I steal by lawns
      and grassy plots,
I slide by hazel
              covers;
I move the sweet
          forget-me-nots
That grow for
          happy lovers.

I slip, I slide,
          I gloom, I glance,
Among my
          skimming swallows;
I make the nettled sunbeam dance
          Against my sandy shallows.

I murmur under moon
              and stars
      In brambly wildernesses;
      I linger by my shingly bars;
I loiter round
          my cresses;

Mouth of the Rivulet.

And out again I curve and flow
To join the brimming river,
For men may come and men may go,
But I go on for ever.

A. Tennyson.

"As the flight of a river
    that flows to the sea,
My soul rushes ever in tumult to thee.
    A two-fold existence, I am where thou art,
        My heart in the distance beats close to thy heart;

Look up, I am near thee, I gaze on thy face,
I see thee, I hear thee, I feel thine embrace."

LORD LYTTON.

L G LAWRENCE. 1890

SUNRISE

"I stood upon the hills, when heaven's wide arch
Was glorious with the sun's
                    returning march,
And woods were brightened, and soft gales
              Went forth to kiss the sun-clad vales."

H. W. LONGFELLOW.

OH, happy day,
I refuse to go!
Hang in the
heavens for
ever so!
For ever in mid-afternoon,
Ah, happy day of happy June!
Pour out thy sunshine on the h
The piny wood with perfume fill,
And breathe across the
singing sea
Land-scented breezes,
that shall be
Sweet as the gardens
that they pass,
Where children tumble in
the grass!

Ah, happy day, refuse to go!
Hang in the heavens
for ever so!
And long not for thy blushing rest
In the soft-bosom of the west;
But bid gray evening get her back
With all the stars upon her track!
Forget the dark, forget the dew,
The mystery of the midnight blue,
And only spread thy wide warm wings
While summer her enchantment flings!

H. P. SPOFFORD.

CARISBROOKE CASTLE.

If thou art worn and hard beset With sorrows, that thou wouldst forget,
If thou wouldst read a lesson, that will keep Thy heart from fainting
and thy soul from sleep,
Go to the woods and hills!—No tears
Dim the sweet look that Nature wears.   H. W. LONGFELLOW.

Christis all.

"Jesus, Refuge of my soul,
    Let me to Thy bosom fly,
While the raging waters roll;
    While the tempest still is high!
Hide me, O my Saviour, hide,
    Till the storm of life be past;
Safe into the haven guide;
    Oh receive my soul at last.

Other refuge have I none,
    Hangs my helpless soul on Thee!
Leave, ah! leave me not alone,
    Still support and comfort me!
All my trust, on Thee is stayed;
    All my help from Thee I bring;
Cover my defenceless head
    With the shadow of Thy wing."

C. Wesley.

" He maketh the storm a calm,
so that the waves thereof are still.

Then are they glad because they be quiet;
so He bringeth them unto their
desired haven. "

Psalm 107: 29 & 30.

Away to the woods.

Away to the woods, away;
All nature is smiling,
        Our young hearts beguiling,
Oh, we will be happy to-day.
Away, away, away, away,
        Away to the woods, away.

As free as the air are we;
        Then rally, then rally,
            From hill-top and valley,
And join in our innocent glee.

We all of us love the school;
        And 'tis in well-doing
        We're pleasure pursuing,
For truth is our guide and our rule.

Success to the school we love,
        It sweetens employment
        With harmless enjoyment,
And trains for the kingdom above.
Away, away, away, away,
        Away to the woods, away.

Rev. A. A. Graley.

"In ripening Summer,
 the full laden vales
Give prospect of employment for
 the flails;
Each breath of wind the bearded
 groves makes bend,
Which seems the fatal sickle
 to portend."

J. Thomson.

"Lift up your eyes,
and look on
the fields,

That they are white
already unto harvest."

S. John, 4: 35. R.V.

Daylight and Moonlight.

In broad daylight, and at noon
  Yesterday I saw the moon
Sailing high, but faint and white,
  As a schoolboy's paper kite.

In broad daylight yesterday,
  I read a Poet's mystic lay;
And it seemed to me at most
  As a phantom, or a ghost.

But at length the feverish day
  Like a passion died away,
And the night, serene and still,
  Fell on village, vale, and hill.

Then the moon, in all her pride,
  Like a spirit glorified,
Filled and overflowed the night
  With revelations of her light.

And the Poet's song again
  Passed like music through
    my brain;
Night interpreted to me
  All its grace and mystery.

H. W. Longfellow.

When the
last sunshine of
expiring day
In summer's twilight weeps itself
away,
Who hath not felt
the softness of the hour
Sink on the heart,
as dew along the flower?"

Lord Byron.

THE POND. BONCHURCH.

Morning.

Day had awakened all things that be,
The lark and the thrush and
the swallow free;
And the milkmaid's song and the mower's scythe,
And the matin-bell and the mountain bee:
Fireflies were quenched on the dewy corn,
Glow-worms went out on the river's brim,
Like lamps which a student forgets to trim,
The beetle forgot to wind his horn, The crickets were still in the meadow and hill:
Like a flock of rooks at a farmer's gun Night's dreams and
Fled from the brains   terrors, everyone,
which are their prey, From the lamp's death
to the morning ray.

SHELLEY.

"Hark! the lark at
heaven's gate sings."
SHAKSPEARE.

The Spirit of Poetry.

TRERIEFE AVENUE, PENZANCE.

Lynmouth.
Cascade at the Waters Meet.

THERE is a quiet spirit in these woods,
That dwells where'er the gentle south wind blows;
Where, underneath the white-thorn, in the glade,
The wild-flowers bloom, or, kissing the soft air,
The leaves above their sunny palms outspread.
With what a tender and impassioned voice
It fills the nice and delicate ear of thought,

When the fast-ushering star of Morning comes
O'er-riding the grey hills with golden scarf;
Or when the cowled and dusky-sandaled Eve,
In mourning weeds, from out the western gate,
Departs with silent pace! That spirit moves
In the green valley, where the silver brook,
From its full laver, pours the white cascade;
And, babbling low amid the tangled woods,
Slips down through moss-grown stones with endless laughter.
And frequent, on the everlasting hills,
Its feet go forth, when it doth wrap itself
In all the dark embroidery of the storm,
And shouts the stern, strong wind. And here, amid
The silent majesty of these deep woods,
Its presence shall uplift thy thoughts from earth,
As to the sunshine and the pure, bright air
Their tops the green trees lift.   Hence gifted bards
Have ever loved the calm and quiet shades.
For them there was an eloquent voice in all
The sylvan pomp of woods, the golden sun,
The flowers, the leaves, the river on its way,
Blue skies, and silver clouds, and gentle winds,—
The swelling upland, where the sidelong sun
Aslant the wooded slope, at evening, goes,—
Groves, through whose broken roof the sky looks in,
Mountain, and shattered cliff, and sunny vale,
The distant lake, fountains, and mighty trees,
In many a lazy syllable, repeating
Their old poetic legends to the wind.

And this is the sweet spirit, that doth fill
The world; and, in these wayward days of youth,
My busy fancy oft embodies it,
As a bright image of the light and beauty
That dwell in nature,—of the heavenly forms
We worship in our dreams, and the soft hues
That stain the wild bird's wing, and flush the clouds
When the sun sets. Within her eye
The heaven of April, with its changing light,
And when it wears the blue of May, is hung,
And on her lip the rich, red rose. Her hair Is like the summer tresses of the trees,
When twilight makes them brown, and on her cheek
Blushes the richness of an autumn sky,
With ever-shifting beauty. Then her breath, It is so like the gentle air of Spring,
As, from the morning's dewy flowers, it comes
Full of their fragrance, that it is a joy
To have it round us,—and her silver voice Is the rich music of a summer bird,
Heard in the still night, with its passionate cadence.

H. W. LONGFELLOW.

Ecclesbourne Glen,
Hastings.

"Pleasant it was, when woods were green,
    And winds were soft and low,
To lie amid some sylvan scene,
    Where, the long drooping boughs between,
Shadows dark and sunlight sheen
    Alternate come and go;
Or, where the denser grove receives
    No sunlight from above,
But the dark foliage interweaves
    In one unbroken roof of leaves,
Underneath whose sloping eaves
    The shadows hardly move."

H. W. LONGFELLOW.

CARNANTON WOODS. S. MAWGAN.

O my
garden full of singing
From the birds that house therein,
Sweet notes down the sweet day
                              ringing
THINK! the shadow on   Till the nightingales
            the dial   begin!
    For the nature most undone,
        Marks the passing of
                the trial,
        Proves the presence of the sun!

                        Mrs. Browning.

Autumn.

Oh what a glory comes and goes the year! The buds of spring, those beautiful harbingers Of sunny skies and cloudless times, enjoy Life's newness, and earth's garniture spread out; And when the silver habit of the clouds Comes down upon the autumn sun, and with A sober gladness the old year takes up His bright inheritance of golden fruits, A pomp and pageant fill the splendid scene. There is a beautiful spirit breathing now Its mellow richness on the clustered trees, And, from a beaker full of richest dyes, Pouring new glory on the autumn woods, And dipping in warm light the pillard clouds. Morn on the mountain, like a summer bird, Lifts up her purple wing, and in the vales

The gentle wind,
a sweet and
passionate wooer,
Kisses the
blushing leaf,
and stirs up life
Within the solemn woods
of ash deep-crimsoned,
And silver beech, and maple
yellow-leaved,
Where autumn, like a faint old man, sits down
By the wayside a-weary. Through the trees
The golden robin moves. The purple finch,
That on wild cherry and red cedar feeds,
A winter bird, comes with its plaintive
whistle,
And pecks by the witch-hazel,
whilst aloud
From cottage roofs the
warbling blue-bird sings,
And merrily, with oft-repeated stroke,
Sounds from the threshing-floor the busy flail.

O what a glory doth this world put on
For him who, with a fervent heart, goes forth
Under the bright and glorious sky, and looks
On duties well performed, and days well spent!

For him the wind, ay, and the yellow leaves,
Shall have a voice, and give him
eloquent teachings.
He shall so hear the solemn hymn,
that Death
Has lifted up for all, that he shall go
To his long resting-place
without a tear.

H. W. LONGFELLOW.

Brightly shines the
Sabbath day,
Calm and peaceful is the morn,
As the farmer wends his way
Through the sheaves
of golden corn.

Six days fall the ripened ears,
Fields are crowned with sheaf
on sheaf;
Then the Sabbath day
appears
For the labourer's relief.

See the sheaves in goodly rows
Glistening in the autumn sun;
Oh, what thanks the farmer owes For the great things God has done.

Happy he who stays his hand, Both in soul and substance blest,
And obeys the Lord's command Even in harvest time to rest.

Happy he who gladly leaves Liberal gleanings to the poor,
Nor sweeps all his golden sheaves
Into his own threshing floor.

From the corners of his field*
He will not clean riddance make
But to God a portion yield
For the poor and stranger's sake.

Every sheaf poor widows glean
From a Christian's fruitful ground
Shall in heavenly barns
          be seen,
And to his account abound.

God remembers those above
Who His Word remember here,
Who His Sabbaths keep and love,
          And His poor relieve and cheer.

Blest their name and home shall be,
     Blest their basket and their store,
          God's salvation they shall see,
               Blest in heaven for evermore!

R. WILTON. M.A.

* "When ye reap the harvest of your land, thou shalt not
make clean riddance of the corners of thy field when
thou reapest, neither shalt thou gather any gleaning
of thy harvest: thou shalt leave them unto the
poor, and to the stranger: I am the Lord your God."

"When ye reap the harvest of your land, thou shalt
not wholly reap the corners of thy field,
neither shalt thou gather the gleanings
of thy harvest."

LEVITICUS, XXIII. 22. and XIX. 9.

"Observe
          How soon the golden field
                    abounds with sheaves;
How soon the
          oat and bearded barley fall,
In frequent lines before the keen-edged scythe;
The clattering team then comes, the
                    swarthy hind
Down leaps and doffs his frock alert and plies
          The shining fork."

HURDIS.

Bonchurch.
The old church.

"Safe, safe upon the
ever-shining shore,
Sin, pain, and death,
and sorrow, all are o'er;
Happy now and
evermore,
Washed in the blood
of the Lamb."

God's-Acre.

God's-Acre.

I like that ancient Saxon phrase, which calls
The burial-ground God's-Acre! It is just;
It consecrates each grave within its walls,
And breathes a benison o'er the sleeping dust.

God's-Acre! Yes, that blessed name imparts
Comfort to those who in the grave have sown
The seed, that they had garnered in their hearts,
Their bread of life, alas! no more their own.

Into its furrows shall we all be cast,
In the sure faith that we shall rise again
At the great harvest, when the archangel's blast
Shall winnow, like a fan, the chaff and grain.

Then shall the good stand in immortal bloom,
In the fair gardens of that second birth;
And each bright blossom mingle its perfume
With that of flowers, which never bloomed on earth.

With thy rude ploughshare, Death, turn up the sod,
And spread the furrow for the seed we sow;
This is the field and Acre of our God,
This is the place where human harvests grow.

H. W. LONGFELLOW.

Abide with me, fast falls the eventide:
The darkness thickens: Lord, with me abide.
When other helpers fail, and comforts flee, Help of the helpless, O abide with me.

Swift to its close ebbs out life's little day; Earth's joys grow dim, its glories pass away;
Change and decay in all around I see: O Thou who changest not, abide with me.

Not a brief glance I beg, a passing word, But as Thou dwell'st with Thy disciples, Lord:
Familiar, condescending, patient, free, Come not to sojourn, but abide with me.

Come not in terrors, as the Kings of kings, But kind and good, with healing in Thy wings;
Tears for all woes, a heart for every plea; Come, Friend of sinners, thus abide with me.

I need Thy presence every passing hour;
What but Thy grace can foil the tempter's power?
Who like Thyself my guide and stay can be? Through cloud and sunshine,
O abide with me.

I fear no foe, with Thee at hand to bless, Ills have no weight, and tears no bitterness.
Where is Death's sting? where, Grave, thy victory? I triumph still, if Thou abide with me.

Reveal Thyself before my closing eyes, Shine through the gloom, and
point me to the skies:
Heaven's morning breaks, and earth's vain shadows flee:
In life, in death, O Lord, abide with me.

H. F. Lyte.

" Until the day break,

and the shadows
flee away. "

Solomon's Song. 2:17.

Land's End.

" Ye were as sheep going astray;
but are now returned. "

I. Peter, II. 25.

I was a wandering sheep,
  I did not love the fold;
I did not love my Shepherd's
          voice,
  I would not be controlled.
I was a wayward child,
  I did not love my home,
I did not love my Father's voice,
  I loved afar to roam.

Jesus my Shepherd is;
  'Twas He that loved my soul,
'Twas He that washed me
          in His blood,
  'Twas He that made me whole.
'Twas He that sought the lost,
  That found the wandering sheep;
'Twas He that brought me to the fold,
  'Tis He that still doth keep.

The Shepherd sought His
          sheep,
  The Father sought His
          child;
They followed me o'er vale and hill,
  O'er deserts waste and wild.
They found me nigh to death,
  Famished, and faint, and lone;
They bound me with the bands
          of love,
  They saved the wandering one.

I was a wandering sheep,
  I would not be controlled,
But now I love my Shepherd's
          voice,
  I love, I love the fold!
I was a wayward child,
  I once preferred to roam;
But now I love
          my Father's voice,
  I love,
          I love His home!

H. BONAR.

Linger, O gentle Time!

Linger, O radiant grace of bright To-day!
Let not the hours' chime
Call thee away,
But linger near me still with fond delay.

Linger, for thou art mine!
What dearer treasures can the future hold?
What sweeter flowers than thine
Can she unfold?
What secrets tell my heart thou hast not told.

Oh linger in thy flight!
For shadows gather round, and should we part
A dreary, starless night
May fill my heart —
Then pause and linger yet, ere thou depart.

Adelaide Procter.

" **All my springs**
                     are in **Thee.** "

Psalm. 87: 7.

" It is from hills that rivers wind,
    Enriching all their course —
        And so, with happy lives — we find
            They have a lofty source. "

EDEN HOOPER.

"As down in the sunless retreats of the ocean,
   Sweet flowers are springing no
                           mortal can see,
So, deep in my soul the still prayer of devotion,
   Unheard by the world,
                       rises silent to Thee,
      My God! silent to Thee —
         Pure, warm, silent to Thee."

THOMAS MOORE.

DOVER CASTLE.

The Lord is my rock and my fortress, and my deliverer, even mine; the God of my rock, in him will I trust; my shield, and the horn of my salvation, my high tower, and my refuge.

2. SAM. XXII. 2. 3. R.V.

To him that overcometh will I grant to sit with me in my throne, even as I also overcame, and am set down with my Father in his throne.

REV. III. 21.

I

Thou art, O God,
the life and light
Of all this wondrous world we see;
Its glow by day, its smile by night, Are but reflections caught from Thee.
Where'er we turn, thy glories shine,
And all things fair and bright are Thine!

III When Night, with wings of starry gloom,
O'ershadows all the earth and skies,
Like some dark, beauteous bird, whose plume
Is sparkling with unnumber'd eyes —
That sacred gloom, those fires divine,
So grand, so countless, Lord! are Thine.

II When Day, with farewell beam, delays
Among the op'ning clouds of Even,
And we can almost think we gaze
Through golden vistas into Heaven —
Those hues that make the Sun's decline
So soft, so radiant, Lord! are Thine.

When youthful Spring around us breathes,
Thy Spirit warms her fragrant sigh;
And ev'ry flower the
Summer wreathes
Is born beneath that
kindling eye.
There'er we turn,
thy glories shine,
And all things
fair and bright
are Thine!

T. Moore.

Grasmere.

GO in peace!
　　　The sun is sinking—
　　Weary breezes die away;
Lo, the threads of sunlight linking
　　Lengthen thro' the woodlands grey!

Tiny rays of golden, peeping
Through the tangles
of the green,
Where the mossy brook is creeping,
While the pathway winds between;

Like the glimpses of a gladness
Such as mortals seldom know,
And an earnest, 'mid our sadness,
Of a joy that will not go.

Often, thus when Day is ending,
And the sunlight falls to rest,
While the sleepy willows bending
Kiss the mere's unruffled breast,

Doth the brightness of the gleaming
Find its way to shady nooks,
Which the noontide's warmest beaming
Could not pierce
with sunny looks.

A. L. SALMON.

Mine be a cot beside a hill,
   A beehive's hum shall soothe my ear;
A willowy brook that turns a mill
With many a fall, shall linger near.

The swallow oft, beneath my thatch,
   Shall twitter from
                  her clay-built nest;
      Oft shall the pilgrim
                  lift the latch
   And share my meal,
                  a welcome guest.

Around my ivied porch shall spring
Each fragrant flower
        that drinks the dew,
And Lucy, at her wheel,
        shall sing
In russet gown and apron blue.

The village church among the trees,
        Where first our marriage vows were given,
With merry peals shall swell the breeze,
        And point with
                taper spire to heaven.

Rogers.

Twilight.

THE twilight is sad
and cloudy,
The wind blows wild
and free,
And like the wings of
sea-birds
Flash the white caps of
the sea.

But in the fisherman's cottage
There shines a ruddier light,
And a little face at the window
Peers out into the night.

Close, close it is pressed to
the window,
As if those childish eyes
Were looking into the darkness,
To see some form arise.

And a woman's waving
shadow
Is passing
to and fro,
Now rising to
the ceiling,
Now bowing and
bending low.

What tale do the roaring ocean,
And the night-wind, bleak and wild,
As they beat at the crazy casement,
Tell to that little child?

And why do the roaring ocean,
And the night-wind, wild and bleak,
As they beat at the heart
of the mother,
Drive the colour from her cheek?

H. W. Longfellow.

"The wind blows wild and free."

Old London Road, Hastings

"This is the day of toil
    Beneath earth's sultry noon,
This is the day of service true,
    But resting cometh soon."

H. BONAR.

The morning time is fresh and fair,
With scent of flowers in the air;
But soon the morning light
is past,
Or overcast.

The evening is the time of peace,
When work is done and
troubles cease,
And sunset lights our
quiet way
At end of day.

E. NESBIT.

Under a spreading
chestnut-tree
The village smithy stands;
The smith, a mighty man is he,
With large and sinewy hands;
And the muscles of
his brawny arms
Are strong as iron bands.

His hair is crisp, and black, and long,
His face is like the tan;
His brow is wet
with honest sweat,
He earns whate'er he can,
He looks the whole world in the face,
For he owes
not any man.

Week in, week out, from morn till night,
You can hear his bellows blow;
You can hear him swing his heavy sledge,
With measured beat and slow,
Like a sexton ringing the village bell,
When the evening sun is low.

And children coming home
                        from school
        Look in at the open door;
They love to see the flaming forge,
        And hear the bellows roar,
        And catch the burning
                        sparks that fly
        Like chaff from a
                        threshing-floor.

He goes on Sunday to the church,
        And sits among his boys;
        He hears the parson pray and preach,
        He hears his daughter's voice,
Singing in the village choir,
        And it makes his
                heart rejoice.

It sounds to him like her
                        mother's voice,
        Singing in Paradise!
He needs must think of her
                        once more,
How in the grave she lies;
        And with his hard, rough
                        hand he wipes
        A tear out of his eyes.

Toiling—rejoicing—
        sorrowing,
    Onward through
            life he goes;
    Each morning sees some task begun,
Each evening sees it close;
    Something attempted, something done,
    Has earned a night's repose.

Thanks, thanks to thee,
            my worthy friend,
    For the lesson thou hast taught!
    Thus at the flaming
                forge of life
Our fortunes must be wrought;
    Thus on its sounding
                anvil shaped
    Each burning
        deed and
            thought.

H. W. Longfellow.

WINTER.

When Winter winds are piercing chill,

And through the hawthorn blows the gale, With solemn feet I tread the hill
That overbrows the lonely vale.

O'er the bare upland, and away Through the long reach of desert woods,
The embracing sunbeams chastely play,
And gladden these deep solitudes.

There, twisted round the barren oak, The summer vine in beauty clung,
And summer winds the stillness broke, The crystal icicle is hung.

There, from their frozen urns, mute springs Pour out the river's gradual tide,
Shrilly the skater's iron rings,
And voices fill the woodland side.

Alas! how changed from the fair scene, When birds sang out their mellow lay,
And winds were soft, and woods were green,
And the song ceased not with the day.

But still wild music is abroad, Pale, desert woods! within your crowd;
And gathering winds, in hoarse accord,
Amid the vocal reeds pipe loud.

Chill airs and wintry winds! my ear Has grown familiar with your song;
I hear it in the opening year,—
I listen, and it
cheers me long.

H. W. LONGFELLOW.

"The embracing sunbeams
chastely play."

Winter.

Though now no more the
          musing ear
     Delights to listen to the breeze,
That lingers   o'er the greenwood shade,
     I love thee, Winter, well.
The green moss shines with icy glare
     The long grass bends its
                    spear-like form
And lovely is the
          silvery scene,
     When faint the sunbeams smile.

R. Southey.

Snow-Flakes.

Out of the bosom of the Air, Out of the cloud-folds of her garments shaken,
     Over the woodlands brown and bare, Over the harvest-fields forsaken,
          Silent, and soft, and slow Descends the snow.

Even as our cloudy fancies take Suddenly shape in some divine expression,
     Even as the troubled heart doth make In the white countenance confession,
          The troubled sky reveals The grief it feels.

This is the poem of the Air, Slowly in silent syllables recorded;
     This is the secret of despair, Long in its cloudy bosom hoarded,
          Now whispered and revealed
               To wood and field.

H. W. Longfellow.

How soft the music
of those village bells,
Falling at intervals upon the ear
In cadence sweet;
now dying all away,
Now pealing loud again, and
louder still.
. . . .
At noon,
Upon the southern side of the
slant hills,
And where the woods fence off
the northern blast,
The season smiles, resigning all its rage,
And has the warmth of May. The vault is blue
Without a cloud, and white without a speck

The dazzling splendour of the scene below.
Again the harmony comes o'er the vale;
And through the trees I view th' embattled tower,
Whence all the music. I again perceive
The soothing influence of the wafted strains,
And settle in soft musings as I tread
The walk, still verdant, under oak and elms.
The redbreast warbles still, but is content
With slender notes, and more than half
suppressed
Pleased with his solitude, and
flitting light
From spray to spray, where'er he
nest he shakes
From many a twig the
pendent drops of ice,
That tinkle in the withered leaves below.

THE CURTAIN OF THE DARK.

THE curtain of the dark
        Is pierced by many a rent:
             Out of the star-wells, spark on spark
            Trickles through night's torn tent.

GRIEF is a tattered tent,
        Where through
             God's light doth shine.
    Who glances up at every rent
        Shall catch a ray divine.

LARCOM.

Lead, Kindly Light,
amid the encircling gloom,
Lead Thou me on:
The night is dark, and I am far from home,
Lead Thou me on:
Keep Thou my feet; I do not ask to see
The distant scene;
one step enough for me.

I was not ever thus, nor prayed that Thou
Shouldst lead me on:
I loved to choose and see my path, but now
Lead Thou me on:
I loved the garish day, and, spite of fears,
Pride ruled my will;
remember not past years.

So long Thy power hath blest me, sure it still
Will lead me on
O'er moor and fen,
o'er crag and torrent, till
The night is gone,
And with the morn those angel faces smile,
Which I have loved long since,
and lost awhile.

J. H. NEWMAN.

My Father's at the Helm.

The curling waves with awful roar,

A gallant ship assailed,

And pallid fear's distracting power

O'er all on board prevailed;

Save one—the captain's darling child,
 Who steadfast viewed the storm;
And, fearless, with composure smiled
 At danger's threatening form.

"And fear'st thou not," a seaman cried,
 "While terrors overwhelm?"—
"Why should I fear?" the boy replied,
 "My father's at the helm."

Thus when our worldly hopes are reft,
 Our earthly comforts gone,
We still have one sure anchor left,—
 God helps, and he alone.

He to our cries will lend an ear;
 He gives our pangs relief;
He turns to smiles each trembling tear,
 To joy each torturing grief.

Then turn to him, 'mid terrors wild,
 When sorrows overwhelm,
Rememb'ring, like the fearless child,
 Our Father's at the helm.

"The darkness falls
from the wings
of Night."

The Day is done.

The day is done, and the darkness
　　Falls from the wings of Night,
As a feather is wafted downward
　　From an eagle in his flight.

I see the lights of the village
　　Gleam through the rain and
　　　　　　the mist,
And a feeling of sadness comes o'er me,
　　That my soul cannot resist:

A feeling of sadness and longing,
　　That is not akin to pain,
And resembles sorrow only
　　As the mist resembles the rain.

Come, read to me some poem,
　　Some simple and heartfelt lay,
That shall soothe this restless feeling,
　　And banish the thoughts of day.

Not from the grand old masters,
　　Not from the bards sublime,
Whose distant footsteps echo
　　Through the corridors of Time.

For, like strains of martial music,
　　Their mighty thoughts suggest
Life's endless toil and endeavour;
　　And to-night I long for rest.

Read from some humbler poet,
　　Whose songs gushed from his heart,
As showers from the clouds
　　　　　　of summer,
　　Or tears from the eyelids start;

Who, through long days of labour,
　　And nights devoid of ease,
Still heard in his soul the music
　　Of wonderful melodies.

Such songs have power to quiet
　　The restless pulse of care,
And come like the benediction
　　That follows after prayer.

Then read from the treasured volume
　　The poem of thy choice,
And lend to the rhyme of the poet
　　The beauty of thy voice.

And the night shall be filled with music,
　　And the cares that infest the day,
Shall fold their tents, like the Arabs,
　　And as silently steal away.

H. W. Longfellow.

"Flying to kiss
a fair lady's cheek."

BEAUTIFUL SNOW.

OH! the snow, the beautiful snow,
　　Filling the sky and the earth below.
　Over the housetops, over the streets,
　　Over the heads of the people you meet;
Dancing— flirting— skimming along,
　Beautiful snow! it can do no wrong;
　　Flying to kiss a fair lady's cheek,
Clinging to lips in frolicsome freak;
　　Beautiful snow from heaven above,
　　Pure as an angel, gentle as love!

Oh! the snow, the beautiful snow,
How the flakes gather
                    and laugh as they go,
Whirling about in maddening fun;
Chasing—laughing—
                    hurrying by,
It lights on the face, and it sparkles the eye;
And the dogs with a bark and a bound
Snap at the crystals as they eddy around;
The town is alive, and its heart in a glow,
To welcome the coming
            of beautiful snow!

How wild the crowd goes swaying along,
   Hailing each other with humour

                              and song:
   How the gay sleighs like meteors flash by,
      Bright for the moment then lost to the eye;
Ringing—swinging—
                  dashing they go,
   Over the crust of
         the beautiful snow;
Snow so pure when it falls from the sky,
   To be trampled and tracked
            by a thousand feet,
Till it blends with filth
      in the horrible street.

ONCE I was pure as the snow, but I fell,
  Fell like the snow-flakes from heaven to hell;
Fell to be trampled as filth on the street,
  Fell to be scoffed, to be spit on and beat;
    Pleading—cursing—dreading to die,
Selling my soul to whoever would buy;
  Dealing in shame for a morsel of bread,
Hating the living and fearing the dead.
    Merciful God, have I fallen so low?
    And yet I was once like the beautiful snow.

ONCE I was fair as the beautiful snow,
    With an eye like a crystal, a heart like its glow,
Once I was loved for my innocent grace—
    Flattered and sought for the charms of my face;
      Fathers,—mothers,—sisters,—all,
God and myself I have lost by my fall;
    The veriest wretch that goes shivering by,
Will make a wide sweep lest I wander too nigh;
    For all that is on or around me I know,
    There is nothing so pure as the beautiful snow.

How strange it should be that this beautiful snow,
Should fall on a sinner with nowhere to go!
How strange it should be when the night comes again,
If the snow and the ice struck my desperate brain,
Fainting,—freezing,—
dying alone,

"How The Gay Sleighs Like Meteors Flash By."

Too wicked for prayer, too weak for a moan,
To be heard in the streets of the crazy town,
Gone mad in the joy of snow coming down;
To be and to die in my terrible woe,
With a bed and a shroud of the beautiful snow.

HELPLESS and foul as
        the trampled snow,
Sinner, despair not! Christ stoopeth low
    To rescue the soul
            that is lost in sin,
And raise it to life and enjoyment again.
    Groaning—bleeding,—
                dying for thee,
The Crucified hung on the cursèd tree!
    His accents of mercy fell soft on thine ear,
    "Is there mercy for me?
                Will He heed my weak prayer?"
O God! in the stream that for sinners did flow,
    Wash me, and I shall be whiter than snow.

MAJOR W. A. H. SIGOURNEY.

GLEN BIRNAM.

THE LIGHT OF OTHER DAYS.

OFT in the stilly night
    Ere slumber's chain has bound me,
Fond Memory brings the light
    Of other days around me:
The smiles, the tears
    Of boyhood's years,
The words of love then spoken;
The eyes that shone,
    Now dimm'd and gone,
The cheerful hearts now broken!
Thus in the stilly night
    Ere slumber's chain has bound me,
Sad Memory brings the light
    Of other days around me.

"O Light of light, shine in!
    Cast out this night of sin;
    Create true day within:
    O Light of light, shine in!"

" Fear was within the tossing bark,
    When stormy winds grew loud,
And waves came rolling high and dark,
    And the tall mast was bowed:

And men stood breathless in their dread,
    And baffled in their skill:
But One was there who rose, and said
    To the wild sea—"Be still!"

F. D. Hemans.

Fierce was the wild billow,
        Dark was the night,
Oars laboured heavily,
        Foam glimmered white;

Trembled the mariners,
        Peril was nigh,
Then said the
        Lord our God,
    Peace, it is I!

Ridge of the
mountain wave,
Lower thy crest;
Wail of the tempest-wind,
Be thou at rest;
Peril can never be,
Sorrow must fly,
Where saith the
Light of light,
Peace, it is I!

Jesus, Deliverer,
Come Thou to me;
Smoothe Thou my voyaging
Over life's sea!
Thou, when the storm of death
Roars, sweeping by,
Whisper, O Truth of truth,
Peace, it is I!

ANATOLIUS. 458.

Lizard Head
and Lights.

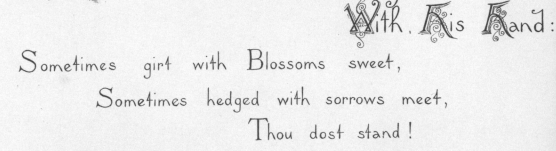

Year by Year
    He leadeth thee
Step by Step,
   so tenderly
      With His Hand:

Sometimes girt with Blossoms sweet,
    Sometimes hedged with sorrows meet,
        Thou dost stand!

Still the Lord of Power is near
    Shielding thee from every fear
        With His Love—

    Follow on then trustfully,
        Meet thy trials cheerfully,
            Rest above!

CECILIA HAVERGAL.

WANDERING SHEEP.

NIGHT-long the flock
  had wandered,
All homeless and forlorn;
 But their Shepherd sought and found them,
    On a snowy Winter morn.

 And now He guides them homeward,
  With gentle voice and hand,
 Even as Ours will guide us
 To His fold in the better land.

A WINTER SONG.

ALAS! cold earth, dost thou forget
  The scent of April's violet?
 Do wailing winds bemoan the death
 Of youth and joy and odorous breath?
Are all these shrivelled leaves that fall
Heaped up for beauty's burial?—

 Ah! no, no, no. The careful year
 Provides a bed, and not a bier;
  Though beauty's trance be long and deep,
  Her heart still quivers in her sleep;—
Then leave her place of slumber bare,
Let the loved sunlight enter there.

CURFEW.

Solemnly, mournfully,
    Dealing its dole,
The Curfew Bell
    Is beginning to toll.

Cover the embers,
    And put out the light;
Toil comes with the morning,
    And rest with the night.

Dark grow the windows,
    And quenched is the fire,
Sound fades into silence,—
    All footsteps retire.

No voice in the chambers,
    No sound in the hall!
Sleep and oblivion
    Reign over all.

The book is completed,
    And closed, like the day;
And the hand that has
                written it
        Lays it away.
Dim grow its fancies,
    Forgotten they lie;
Like coals in the ashes,
    They darken and die.

Song sinks into silence,
    The story is told,
The windows are darkened,
    The hearth-stone is cold.

Darker and darker
    The black shadows fall;
Sleep and oblivion
    Reign over all.

H. W. LONGFELLOW.